Platero y yo

Platero and I

Platero y yo

Platero and I

by JUAN RAMÓN JIMÉNEZ

Selected, translated, and adapted from the Spanish
by Myra Cohn Livingston and Joseph F. Domínguez

Illustrations by Antonio Frasconi

CLARION BOOKS · NEW YORK

Clarion Books
a Houghton Mifflin Company imprint
215 Park Avenue South, New York, NY 10003
Text copyright © 1957 by Juan Ramón Jiménez
English translation copyright © 1994 by Myra Cohn Livingston
and Joseph F. Domínguez
Illustrations copyright © 1994 by Antonio Frasconi

Illustrations executed in full-color woodcuts and mixed media
Text is Galliard Roman
For information about permission to reproduce selections from
this book, write to Permissions, Houghton Mifflin Company,
215 Park Avenue South, New York, NY 10003.
Printed in the USA
Book design and typography by Carol Goldenberg

Library of Congress Cataloging-in-Publication Data
Jiménez, Juan Ramón, 1881–1958.
   [Platero y yo.   English.   Selections]
   Platero / selections from Platero y yo by Juan Ramón Jiménez;
translated by Myra Cohn Livingston and Joseph F. Domínguez;
illustrated by Antonio Frasconi.
      p.   cm.
   Summary: Presents a picture of life in the town of Moguer, in
Andalusia, Spain, as seen through the eyes of a wandering poet and
his faithful donkey. Text in English and Spanish.
   ISBN 0-395-62365-0
   [1. Andalusia (Spain)—Social life and customs.   2. Spain—Social
life and customs.   3. Donkeys.   4. Spanish language materials—
Bilingual.]   I. Frasconi, Antonio, ill.   II. Title.
PQ6619.I4P633   1993
863'.62—dc20   92-11634
                                                          CIP
                                                           AC

HOR 10 9 8 7 6 5 4 3 2 1

Contents ❧

Platero 🐝

Platero es pequeño, peludo, suave; tan blando por fuera, que se diría todo de algodón, que no lleva huesos. Sólo los espejos de azabache de sus ojos son duros cual dos escarabajos de cristal negro.

Lo dejo suelto, y se va al prado, y acaricia tibiamente con su hocico, rozándolas apenas, las florecillas rosas, celestes y gualdas... Lo llamo dulcemente: «¿Platero?», y viene a mí con un trotecillo alegre que parece que se ríe, en no sé qué cascabeleo ideal...

Come cuanto le doy. Le gustan las naranjas, mandarinas, las uvas moscateles, todas de ámbar, los higos morados, con su cristalina gotita de miel...

Es tierno y mimoso igual que un niño, que una niña...; pero fuerte y seco por dentro, como de piedra. Cuando paso sobre él, los domingos, por las últimas callejas del pueblo, los hombres del campo, vestidos de limpio y despaciosos, se quedan mirándolo:

—Tien' asero...

Tiene acero. Acero y plata de luna, al mismo tiempo.

Platero

Platero is so little, so hairy, smooth, and so soft to the touch that you might say he is made of puffy cotton, all light and boneless. Only do the mirrors of his dark eyes seem to be hard, jet-black, like two beetles, like two scarabs made of brilliant glass.

I turn him loose and he goes off straight to the meadow, fondling, caressing the blossoms, his muzzle barely brushing the tender flowers, sky-blue as the air, golden as the sun, pink and red as the sunrise and sunset. . . . Then softly I call to him, "Platero?" and he comes to me with a happy trot, running with such a merry jingle that it seems to me like a vague tinkling, a laughter he makes . . .

What I give him he eats. He loves the taste of amber-colored muscatel grapes, mandarin oranges, and the deep purple figs as they burst with their crystalline honey, a sweetness of warm, golden drops . . .

He is tender and finicky like a young boy, a small girl, a child . . . but inside he is strong, he is dry like rock, like the land he walks. When I ride him on Sundays through the outskirts of the small village, down the streets, the narrow lanes, field men, the strong men, all dressed in their Sunday clothes, stand and look; slowly they watch and speak of him:

"Steel, he's got steel . . ."

Yes, he's got steel. Steel and the silvery sheen of the moonlight, and all at the same time.

Juegos del anochecer 🐌

Cuando, en el crespúsculo del pueblo, Platero y yo entramos, ateridos, por la oscuridad morada de la calleja miserable que da al río seco, los niños pobres juegan a asustarse, fingiéndose mendigos. Uno se echa un saco a la cabeza, otro dice que no ve, otro se hace el cojo...

Después, en ese brusco cambiar de la infancia, como llevan unos zapatos y un vestido, y como sus madres, ellas sabrán cómo, les han dado algo de comer, se creen unos príncipes:

—Mi pare tié un reló e plata.

—Y er mío, un cabayo.

—Y er mío, una ejcopeta.

Reloj que levantará a la madrugada, escopeta que no matará el hambre, caballo que llevará a la miseria...

El corro, luego. Entre tanta negrura, una niña forastera, que habla de otro modo, la sobrina del Pájaro Verde, con voz débil, hilo de cristal acuoso en la sombra, canta entonadamente, cual una princesa:

> *Yo soy laaa viudiiitaaa*
> *del Condeee de Orée...*

... ¡Sí, sí! ¡Cantad, soñad, niños pobres! Pronto, al amanecer vuestra adolescencia, la primavera os asustará, como un mendigo, enmascarada de invierno.

—Vamos, Platero...

4

Games at Dusk ⚘

Shivering with cold at the sunset hour, Platero and I arrive at the small village through a narrow, dirty, miserable street purpled with darkness, which ends in a dry river bed. Here children play at games, frightening each other, pretending they are beggars. One pretends he has only one leg, another throws a sack over his head; one pretends he cannot see . . .

Then suddenly, as children will do, they change their minds and their games. Because their mothers, though heaven knows how, manage to find them some shoes or clothing, to give them a bit of food at home, they make believe they are princes, princesses:

"My dad's got him a watch made of silver."

"And mine's got his own horse."

"And mine, he's got himself a shotgun."

A watch that will waken at daybreak, a shotgun that will not kill his hunger, a horse to carry him further along to misery and poverty . . .

And then they join hands making a circle. Darkness comes. One small girl, different than these children, born far away, the niece of a man they have nicknamed Green Bird, raises her small voice, as feeble, fragile, clear as a slender thread of crystal piercing through the gloom and darkness, and sings like a princess:

> *I am the young widow*
> *of the great Count Oree . . .*

. . . Yes, yes! Sing on, dream on, you poor children. Soon enough, just when you think the dawn of your life will begin, your sweet spring, watch how spring will arrive frightening you, masked like winter, like a beggar.

"Let's go, Platero . . ."

La carretilla 🦋

En el arroyo grande, que la lluvia había dilatado hasta la viña, nos encontramos, atascada, una vieja carretilla, perdida toda bajo su carga de hierba y de naranjas. Una niña, rota y sucia, lloraba sobre una rueda, queriendo ayudar con el empuje de su pechillo en flor al borricuelo, más pequeño ¡ay! y más flaco que Platero. Y el borriquillo se despechaba contra el viento, intentando, inútilmente, arrancar del fango la carreta, al grito sollozante de la chiquilla. Era vano su esfuerzo, como el de los niños valientes, como el vuelo de esas brisas cansadas del verano que se caen, en un desmayo, entre las flores.

Acaricié a Platero y, como pude, lo enganché a la carretilla, delante del borrico miserable. Le obligué, entonces, con un cariñoso imperio, y Platero, de un tirón, sacó carretilla y rucio del atolladero, y les subió la cuesta.

¡Qué sonreír el de la chiquilla! Fue como si el sol de la tarde, que se quebraba, al ponerse entre las nubes de agua, en amarillos cristales, le encendiese una aurora tras sus tiznadas lágrimas.

Con su llorosa alegría, me ofreció dos escogidas naranjas, finas, pesadas, redondas. Las tomé, agradecido, y le di una al borriquillo débil, como dulce consuelo; otra a Platero, como premio áureo.

The Little Cart ❧

In the big creek all swollen by the rain, flooded up almost as far as the vineyard, Platero and I came across, stuck there deep in the mud and mire, an old worn-out cart, almost lost to view under its load of grass and oranges. Sobbing, weeping over one wheel of the cart, a young girl, ragged, dirty, was pushing with her budding breasts against the cart, trying to help her sad, little donkey; a donkey, alas, smaller, frailer, and thinner than Platero. And the little burro was pulling, pushing, pushing his chest against the wind, trying futilely to pull the cart from the mud, to the sobbing and uncontrollable crying of the young girl. All in vain, the donkey's courage like that of the bravado children, like that of cool fluttering breezes that waft hopefully in summer, yet fall down discouraged, tired, into the flowers.

Patting Platero, I hitched him as well as I was able to the sunken, muddy cart, just ahead of the little, sad donkey. Encouraging him then, with a most affectionate command, I spoke, and Platero, with one tug, pulled the cart and the donkey and brought them up out of the deep, flooded creek, up from the mire, and then up along the incline.

What a smile on the face of the child! It was as though the sun, at evening, hidden behind clouds of rain, setting among them, were breaking up into crystals of yellow, burning through and kindling behind her smudgy tears a new light, a shining dawn.

Through brimming eyes now shone happiness as she carefully chose and offered me two oranges, perfect oranges, round and heavy, and with gratitude I accepted them, and to the frail little donkey I gave one as a token of sweet comfort, and to Platero the other, a golden prize.

El pan 🐛

Te he dicho, Platero, que el alma de Moguer es el vino, ¿verdad? No; el alma de Moguer es el pan. Moguer es igual que un pan de trigo, blanco por dentro, como el migajón, y dorado en torno—¡oh sol moreno!—como la blanda corteza.

A mediodía, cuando el sol quema más, el pueblo entero empieza a humear y a oler a pino y a pan calentito. A todo el pueblo se le abre la boca. Es como una gran boca que come un gran pan. El pan se entra en todo: en el aceite, en el gazpacho, en el queso y la uva, para dar sabor a beso, en el vino, en el caldo, en el jamón, en él mismo, pan con pan. También solo, como la esperanza, o con una ilusión...

Los panaderos llegan trotando en sus caballos, se paran en cada puerta entornada, tocan las palmas y gritan: «¡El panaderooo!»... Se oye el duro ruido tierno de los cuarterones que, al caer en los canastos que brazos desnudos levantan, chocan con los bollos, de las hogazas con las roscas...

Y los niños pobres llaman, al punto, a las campanillas de las cancelas o a los picaportes de los portones, y lloran largamente hacia adentro: ¡Un poquiiito de paaan!...

The Bread ❧

I have told you, Platero, haven't I, that the soul of Moguer is in its wine? No, the soul of our village is its bread. Moguer is the same as a loaf of wheat bread, white on the inside and filled with tender dough, while the outside is golden—oh, brown like the sun!—golden and brown and all crusty.

When noon comes, when the sun burns its brightest, a warm smoke rises, enveloping our village, and the village starts to smell of pinewood and of bread warmly rising. Then all of the village opens up like a huge mouth; it is like one enormous mouth eating a large loaf.

The bread gives life to everything. It goes with oil and with gazpacho and with cheese and with the grapes; it gives to a kiss a sweet flavoring; it goes with wine and with soup and broth and with ham and with itself, bread with bread. Also, when eaten alone, it brings hope, it brings illusion and dreaming . . .

The baker boys begin to arrive on their trotting horses and stop at the front of every half-closed doorway, clapping their hands and calling, "The baaakerrrr!" . . . And then you can hear the plopping, the hard sound of the quarter loaves as they fall into the baskets, held there by upraised bare arms, hear the crashing of the small loaves and buns against the ring-shaped loaves, quarter loaves.

Then, immediately, poor hungry children ring the outer doorbells at iron gratings, jiggle the clanging latches of heavy locked doors, and cry, the echoes resounding through the corridors: Just a litttttttle brrread . . .

Amistad 🙢

Nos entendemos bien. Yo lo dejo ir a su antojo, y él me lleva siempre adonde quiero.

Sabe Platero que, al llegar al pino de la Corona, me gusta acercarme a su tronco y acariciárselo, y mirar el cielo al través de su enorme y clara copa; sabe que me deleita la veredilla que va, entre céspedes, a la Fuente vieja; que es para mí una fiesta ver el río desde la colina de los pinos, evocadora, con su bosquecillo alto, de parajes clásicos. Como me adormile, seguro, sobre él, mi despertar se abre siempre a uno de tales amables espectáculos.

Yo trato a Platero cual si fuese un niño. Si el camino se torna fragoso y le pesa un poco, me bajo para aliviarlo. Lo beso, lo engaño, lo hago rabiar... Él comprende bien que lo quiero, y no me guarda rencor. Es tan igual a mí, tan diferente a los demás, que he llegado a creer que sueña mis propios sueños.

Platero se me ha rendido como una adolescente apasionada. De nada protesta. Sé que soy su felicidad. Hasta huye de los burros y de los hombres...

Our Friendship 🐛

We understand each other. I let him go wherever he wishes and always he takes me where it is I wish to go.

Only Platero knows, reaching the pine tree of La Corona, what joy it gives me, how tenderly I approach its trunk, caressing it, gazing at blue sky through the opening of light through the dappled tree top. Only he knows the little path which brings me such delight, leading through the meadowland to the Old Fountain; what pleasure it gives me when I can view the river from the forest of trees on the hillside, the tall pines recalling, bringing back to me the deep sweet memories of dreams. If I should sleep, drowse on Platero's back, I know that I will waken always to find myself gazing upon one of these familiar restful scenes.

I always treat Platero as if he were a child. Should the path be too rough or uneven I dismount so his load will be lighter and a bit easier. I kiss him, tease him and trick and tease again . . . Yet he understands well what my wishes are and he bears me no grudge. He is so much like me, so different from the others that I have come now to believe we dream the same . . . his dreams mine . . . and my dreams his.

Platero has abandoned himself, given himself to me with love, like an adolescent. There's nothing he protests. I know I am his happiness, his joy. He even shies away from other men and donkeys . . .

La arrulladora 🎵

La chiquilla del carbonero, bonita y sucia cual una moneda, bruñidos los negros ojos y reventando sangre los labios prietos entre la tizne, está a la puerta de la choza, sentada en una teja, durmiendo al hermanito.

Vibra la hora de mayo, ardiente y clara como un sol por dentro. En la paz brillante, se oye el hervor de la olla que cuece en el campo, la brama de la dehesa de los Caballos, la alegría del viento del mar en la maraña de los eucaliptos.

Sentida y dulce, la carbonera canta:

Mi niiiño se va a dormiii
en graaasia de la Pajtoraaa...

Pausa. El viento en las copas...

...y pooor dormirse mi niñooo,
se duerme la arruyadoraaa...

El viento... Platero, que anda, manso, entre los pinos quemados, se llega, poco a poco... Luego se echa en la tierra fosca y, a la larga copla de madre, se adormila, igual que un niño.

The Lullaby Singer 🙎

The young daughter of the coal seller, as pretty, yet dirty and smudged dark, as a coin, with her shining black eyes and lips bursting red with blood, like coal when it smoulders beneath ashes, sits at the door of a shack on a roofing tile rocking and rocking and singing, crooning to sleep her small baby brother.

Vibrant is May at this hour, fiery clear like the sun within, bursting, brilliant. In this bright tranquility sounds of a pot boiling and bubbling are heard in a nearby field, the low neighing of horses off in their pasture ground, and the far laughter of the sea wind as it tangles through the branches of the eucalyptus.

The coal seller's daughter sings with warm feeling, sweetness:

> *My baby will sleep, will sleep*
> *to please the good, sweet shepherdess, sleep . . .*

Pause. And the wind sings through the tree tops . . .

> *. . . but it is not the small baby*
> *who drowses, it is the singer . . .*

And the wind sings . . . Platero, who very gently and softly walks through the burnt pine trees approaches little by little . . . and comes to a dry pebbled patch of ground, and lies down, and hearing a mother's lullaby falls asleep, as if he were a baby.

El tío de las vistas 🦋

De pronto, sin matices, rompe el silencio de la calle el seco redoble de un tamborcillo. Luego, una voz cascada tiembla un pregón jadeoso y largo. Se oyen carreras, calle abajo... Los chiquillos gritan: ¡El tío de las vistas! ¡Las vistas! ¡Las vistas!

En la esquina, una pequeña caja verde con cuatro banderitas rosas espera sobre su catrecillo, la lente al sol. El viejo toca y toca el tambor. Un grupo de chiquillos sin dinero, las manos en el bolsillo o a la espalda, rodean, mudos, la cajita. A poco, llega otro corriendo, con su perra en la palma de la mano. Se adelanta, pone sus ojos en la lente...

—¡Ahooora se verá... al general Prim... en su caballo blancooo...!—dice el viejo forastero con fastidio, y toca el tambor.

—¡El puerto... de Barcelonaaa...!—Y más redoble.

Otros niños van llegando con su perra lista, y la adelantan al punto al viejo, mirándolo absortos, dispuestos a comprar su fantasía. El viejo dice:

—¡Ahooora se verá... el castillo de la Habanaaa!—Y toca el tambor...

Platero, que se ha ido con la niña y el perro de enfrente a ver las vistas, mete su cabezota por entre las de los niños, por jugar. El viejo, con un súbito buen humor, le dice: ¡Venga tu perra!

Y los niños sin dinero se ríen todos sin ganas, mirando al viejo con una humilde solicitud aduladora...

The Old Man of the Pictures 🐚

The harsh sound, the dull, dry, monotonous sound of a little drum roll is heard, breaking the silence of the street. Soon after, a cracked, broken voice, out of breath, trembling, calls out a long announcement. The pavement resounds with running pounding feet . . . The children cry out: "Here comes the man with the pictures! The pictures! The pictures!"

In the corner a little box of green, decorated with four rose-colored flags, waits enticingly upon a canvas camp stool, its lens toward the sun. The old man beats and beats again on the drum. A group of little children who have no money, their hands down deep in their pockets or behind their backs, silently surround the small box. And soon, another child comes running up, a nickel held out in the palm of his hand. Then, he steps forward, putting his eye close to the lens.

"Nooooooow, you will see . . . General Prim . . . on his whiiiite horse!" yells the old man, his tedious voice filled with weariness, and beats on his drum.

"The harbor . . . of Barcelonaaaa . . . !"—and more drum rolling.

Other children come running up with their nickels ready, and hand the old man their money, hypnotized, watching him with rapt awe, with reverence, eager to buy his make-believe world.

The old man calls again:

"Nnnoooooow you will see . . . the great castle of Havanaaaa!"—and more drum rolling . . .

Platero, who has come to see the peepshow with the little girl and her dog who live across the street, pokes his head, playfully, in between the faces of the children. The old man, in a sudden burst of humor, says to Platero: "Let's have your nickel!"

And the children without money, laughing only to be polite, gaze up at the old man, giving him their meekest, most humble look of adulation . . .

El sello 🎗

Aquél tenía la forma de un reloj, Platero. Se abría la cajita de plata y aparecía, apretado contra el paño de tinta morada, como un pájaro en su nido. ¡Qué ilusión cuando, después de oprimirlo un momento contra la palma blanca, fina y malva de mi mano, aparecía en ella la estampilla:

FRANCISCO RUIZ, *Moguer.*

¡Cuánto soñé yo con aquel sello de mi amigo del colegio de don Carlos! Con una imprentilla que me encontré arriba, en el escritorio viejo de mi casa, intenté formar uno con mi nombre. Pero no quedaba bien, y sobre todo, era difícil la impresión. No era como el otro, que con tal facilidad dejaba, aquí y allá, en un libro, en la pared, en la carne, su letrero:

FRANCISCO RUIZ, *Moguer.*

Un día vino a mi casa, con Arias, el platero de Sevilla, un viajante de escritorio. ¡Qué embeleso de reglas, de compases, de tintas de colores, de sellos! Los había de todas las formas y tamaños. Yo rompí mi alcancía, y con un duro que me encontré, encargué un sello con mi nombre y pueblo. ¡Qué larga semana aquélla! ¡Qué latirme el corazón cuando llegaba el coche del correo! ¡Qué sudor triste cuando se alejaban, en la lluvia, los pasos del cartero! Al fin, una noche, me lo trajo. Era un breve aparato complicado, con lápiz, pluma, iniciales para lacre..., ¡qué sé yo! Y dando a un resorte, aparecía la estampilla, nuevecita, flamante.

¿Quedó algo por sellar en mi casa? ¿Qué no era mío? Si otro me pedía el sello—¡cuidado, que se va a gastar!—, ¡qué angustia! Al día siguiente, ¡con qué prisa alegre llevé al colegio todo!: libros, blusa, sombrero, botas, manos, con el letrero:

JUAN RAMÓN JIMÉNEZ, *Moguer.*

The Rubber Stamp 🕭

That rubber stamp was shaped like a little watch, Platero. You opened up the small box, made of silver, and there it was, pressed close against a pad made of purple ink, just like a tiny bird hiding deep within its colored nest. Oh what a delight, when, upon holding it, just for a moment, pressing it against the white and mauve of the palm of my hand, there it was—the name and the village stamped in purple:

FRANCISCO RUIZ, *Moguer.*

How long I dreamed about that rubber stamp owned by my schoolfriend who went to the school of Don Carlos! And when I discovered, upstairs, in my house, an old worn out desk with a small printing press, how hard I kept trying to make a rubber stamp bearing my own name. But it didn't come out too well, and, worst of all, it didn't give a good clear impression. The pressing was too faint, too difficult, not like the other one, which left clearly, easily, an inked impression, here and there, on a book or on a wall or on one's skin, the purple legend:

FRANCISCO RUIZ, *Moguer.*

One day there came to my house with Arias, a silversmith from Sevilla, a traveling stationery salesman. What a fascinating array of rulers, of compasses, colored inks, rubber stamps! They were made in many shapes, many forms, and all sizes. I cracked my piggy bank open and with a quarter I found, ordered my own rubber stamp with my name and village.

What a long week that was! How my heart beat, how I trembled whenever the mail carrier came with the letters! What a cold sweat, what sadness I felt when the postman's footsteps moved farther off, echoing in the rain. Finally, one night, he delivered it. It was small, a complicated gadget, with a pencil, pen, initials to put on sealing wax, some other stuff . . . and, at the touch of a spring, the stamp sprang up, brand new, shining brightly.

Was anything left unmarked in my house? Was anything not mine? If another kid wanted to borrow it, to use my stamp—careful! You'll wear it out! What anxiety! The following day, with what delight I hurried away to school with everything! Books and shirt, hat and boots, and hands stamped with the legend:

JUAN RAMÓN JIMÉNEZ, *Moguer.*

La perra parida 🦋

La perra de que te hablo, Platero, es la de Lobato, el tirador. Tú la conoces bien, porque la hemos encontrado muchas veces por el camino de los Llanos... ¿Te acuerdas? Aquella dorada y blanca, como un poniente anubarrado de mayo... Parió cuatro perritos, y Salud, la lechera, se los llevó a su choza de las Madres, porque se le estaba muriendo un niño, y don Luis le había dicho que le diera caldo de perritos. Tú sabes bien lo que hay de la casa de Lobato al puente de las Madres, por la pasada de las Tablas...

Platero, dicen que la perra anduvo como loca todo aquel día, entrando y saliendo, asomándose a los caminos, encaramándose en los vallados, oliendo a la gente... Todavía a la oración la vieron, junto a la casilla del celador, en los Hornos, aullando tristemente sobre unos sacos de carbón contra el ocaso.

Tú sabes bien lo que hay de la calle de Enmedio a la pasada de las Tablas... Cuatro veces fue y vino la perra durante la noche, y cada una se trajo a un perrito en la boca, Platero. Y al amanecer, cuando Lobato abrió su puerta, estaba la perra en el umbral mirando dulcemente a su amo, con todos los perritos agarrados, en torpe temblor, a sus tetillas rosadas y llenas...

The Mother Dog 🎗

The bitch I am telling you of, Platero, belongs to Lobato, the sharpshooter. You know her well, because we have come across her and have met her many times along the way on the Llanos road . . . Don't you remember? The one that is golden, gold, and white, much like a cloudy sunset during the month of May, gave birth to four tiny puppies, and Salud, who delivers the milk, took them to her small cabin at Las Madres because one of her children, a small one, was dying, and Don Luis had spoken to her about feeding the child broth, some puppy-dog broth. You know well how far, what a distance it is from Lobato's house to the bridge at Las Madres as you cross the river by La Tablas . . .

Platero, people say the bitch went around like she was half-crazy the whole day long, to and fro, going and coming, searching everywhere among the trails and climbing up on top of the fences, sniffing everyone she met . . . Even when it was time for Vespers, still they saw her close at hand, near the house of the warden there at Los Hornos. She was howling, sorrowfully, sadly, standing there on some stacks of coal, black against the sunset.

You know very well what a long, long way it is from Enmedio Street to the crossing at Las Tablas . . . Four times during the night the bitch went and came back, back and forth, and each time bringing a puppy, and another puppy, in her mouth, Platero. And then, when it was daybreak and Lobato opened his door, she was on the threshold looking at him, her master, with sweetness and love, and there, joined to her, the puppies half-asleep, all four puppies, tremoring and trembling, were suckling her full, rosy teats.

Los fuegos ❧

Para setiembre, en las noches de velada, nos poníamos en el cabezo que hay detrás de la casa del huerto, a sentir el pueblo en fiesta desde aquella paz fragante que emanaban los nardos de la alberca. Pioza, el viejo guarda de viñas, borracho en el suelo de la era, tocaba cara a la luna, hora tras hora, su caracol.

Ya tarde, quemaban los fuegos. Primero eran sordos estampidos enanos; luego, cohetes sin cola, que se abrían arriba, en un suspiro, cual un ojo estrellado que viese, un instante, rojo, morado, azul el campo; y otros cuyo esplendor caía como una doncellez desnuda que se doblara de espaldas, como un sauce de sangre que gotease flores de luz. ¡Oh, qué pavos reales encendidos, qué macizos aéreos de claras rosas, qué faisanes de fuego por jardines de estrellas!

Platero, cada vez que sonaba un estallido, se estremecía, azul, morado, rojo en el súbito iluminarse del espacio; y en la claridad vacilante, que agrandaba y encogía su sombra sobre el cabezo, yo veía sus grandes ojos negros que me miraban asustados.

Cuando, como remate, entre el lejano vocerío del pueblo, subía al cielo constelado la áurea corona giradora del castillo, poseedora del trueno gordo, que hace cerrar los ojos y taparse los oídos a las mujeres, Platero huía entre las cepas, como alma que lleva el diablo, rebuznando enloquecido hacia los tranquilos pinos en sombra.

The Fireworks 🐝

During the holiday nights in September, we used to sit on top of the hill just behind the orchard house, sensing and feeling the villagers' excitement, the gaiety of fiesta, and absorbing all the fragrance that came wafting up to us from the lily pond. Pioza, the old man who tended the vineyards, was drunk and lay stretched out on the threshing field floor, facing toward the moon, blowing, hour after hour, on his shell horn.

The burning of fireworks started late. At first the explosions were short, dull, small cracks, muffled. Immediately after, sky rockets without tails began to open with sighs, and seemed to be like a starry eye that might look down, for an instant, over fields turned red, or blue, or purple; and others, whose burning splendor would seem as they fell like a young, naked maiden, her back arched, shining, bowing to earth, like a blood-red willow leaking flowers of light, drop by drop. Oh, what flaming magnificent peacocks, what great bunches of massed bright roses bloomed overhead, what fiery pheasants in that far, starry garden!

Platero, with each explosion, trembled, turning as blue, as red, as purple as the bursts of color suddenly illuminating the empty, endless outreaches of space. And in those sudden flashes against the hill, I could see his great black eyes, terror-stricken, seeking me, looking at me, frightened.

Then, for a finale, amidst distant sounds of shouting and yelling from the village, when the golden revolving crown of the castle rose up to the sky, twirling and spinning faster and faster, and with it the last blasting explosion, a noise which makes women close their eyes and hold up their hands to cover up their ears, Platero used to run among the vinestock as if the devil were carrying away his soul, braying as though he were crazy, toward the calm pines resting in shadow.

La luna

Platero acababa de beberse dos cubos de agua con estrellas en el pozo del corral, y volvía a la cuadra, lento y distraído, entre los altos girasoles. Yo le aguardaba en la puerta, echado en el quicio de cal y envuelto en la tibia fragancia de los heliotropos.

Sobre el tejadillo, húmedo de las blanduras de setiembre, dormía el campo lejano, que mandaba·un fuerte aliento de pinos. Una gran nube negra, como una gigantesca gallina que hubiese puesto un huevo de oro, puso la luna sobre una colina.

Yo le dije a la luna:

> *...Ma sola*
> *ha questa luna in ciel, che da nessuno*
> *cader fu vista mai se non in sogno.*

Platero la miraba fijamente y sacudía, con un duro ruido blando, una oreja. Me miraba absorto y sacudía la otra...

The Moon 🐚

Platero had just finished drinking two bucketfuls of water, swimming with stars, out of the well in the corral, and was returning, absentmindedly, slowly toward the stable, moving about the tall sunflowers. I was waiting for him, stretched out lazily against the whitewashed door sill, wrapped up and enveloped by the warm fragrance, the sweet smell of the blooming heliotrope.

Over the small roof, dampened, moistened with the mild softness of September, the distant meadows lay sleeping, carrying back to me the pungent aroma of the pine trees. In the sky, one black cloud, reminding me of a gigantic hen, a hen who had laid an enormous golden egg up there—black cloud and hen laying the moon upon the hill—

And I said to the moon:

> *. . . only one moon*
> *up there in the sky, never seen by anyone,*
> *falling, falling, except in a dream.*

Platero was watching the moon, was watching it so intently that one ear began to tremble with a soft, crackling sound. And then, looking pensively at me, he shook the other . . .

Alegría

Platero juega con Diana, la bella perra blanca que se parece a la luna creciente, con la vieja cabra gris, con los niños...

Salta Diana, ágil y elegante, delante del burro, sonando su leve campanilla, y hace como que le muerde los hocicos. Y Platero, poniendo las orejas en punta, cual dos cuernos de pita, la embiste blandamente y la hace rodar sobre la hierba en flor.

La cabra va al lado de Platero, rozándose a sus patas, tirando con los dientes de la punta de las espadañas de la carga. Con una clavellina o con una margarita en la boca, se pone frente a él, le topa en el testuz, y brinca luego, y bala alegremente, mimosa, igual que una mujer...

Entre los niños, Platero es de juguete. ¡Con qué paciencia sufre sus locuras! ¡Cómo va despacito, deteniéndose, haciéndose el tonto, para que ellos no se caigan! ¡Cómo los asusta, iniciando, de pronto, un trote falso!

¡Claras tardes del otoño moguereño! Cuando el aire puro de octubre afila los límpidos sonidos, sube del valle un alborozo idílico de balidos, de rebuznos, de risas de niños, de ladreos y de campanillas...

Happiness ✤

Platero plays with Diana, the white dog so beautiful that she resembles a lovely, slim, crescent moon; plays with the old grey nanny goat, with the children . . .

Nimbly, Diana, agile and elegant, jumps in front of the donkey; her soft little bell is tinkling, ringing. She is pretending to bite his nose, his lips, his muzzle. And Platero, his ears pointed like horns of the moon, like the horns of a fighting bull, charges Diana gently and tumbles her, rolls her in the flowering grass.

The nanny goat walks close to Platero and, brushing against his legs, is pulling with her teeth at the sharp ends of the cattails hanging from his burden. And, with a red carnation or perhaps a daisy held there in her mouth, she stands in front of him, butting him on his forehead, leaping backward and bleating at him softly, flirting, playing with him like a spoiled woman . . .

Among the children Platero is like a toy. With what patience he suffers, enduring their crazy pranks! How slowly he moves about, with what care he stops! How he plays at being the fool, careful, so that they will not fall off his back! How he frightens them from time to time, starting suddenly his false trotting!

Evenings clear and bright in Moguer in the autumn! When all the air is pure in October it sharpens the crystalline, calm, limpid sounds rising up from the valley below; the simple charm of an idyllic merriment of bleatings, brayings, laughter of children, barkings, and bells tinkling . . .

Pasan los patos

He ido a darle agua a Platero. En la noche serena, toda de nubes vagas y estrellas, se oye, allá arriba, desde el silencio del corral, un incesante pasar de claros silbidos.

Son los patos. Van tierra adentro, huyendo de la tempestad marina. De vez en cuando, como si nosotros hubiéramos ascendido o como si ellos hubiesen bajado, se escuchan los ruidos más leves de sus alas, de sus picos, como cuando, por el campo, se oye clara la palabra de alguno que va lejos...

Horas y horas, los silbidos seguirán pasando, en un huir interminable. Platero, de vez en cuando, deja de beber y levanta la cabeza como yo, como las mujeres de Millet, a las estrellas, con una blanda nostalgia infinita...

Passing of the Ducks 🐚

I have gone to give Platero some water. In the silence of night, a night filled with wandering clouds and silver stars, we hear high above, overhead, beyond the stillness of the corral, an incessant sound of clear bright passing whistles.

The wild ducks. Flying, flying inland, fleeing from a tempestuous storm out at sea. From time to time, as though we ourselves had been ascending skyward and upward, or they had descended down, flying back down earthward, we hear the slight rustling, the faint shushing of their wings, the rubbing of bills, as clearly as we can hear the words spoken by someone walking in the field at a great distance . . .

For hours and hours, the whistling passage of the birds will continue, their flight, their escape, endless:

Platero from time to time pauses, stops drinking water and raises his head, just as I do, just as the Millet women do, looking up to the stars with tenderness, with his own unquenchable yearning . . .

El canario se muere 🎵

Mira, Platero: el canario de los niños ha amanecido hoy muerto en su jaula de plata. Es verdad que el pobre estaba ya muy viejo... El invierno último, tú te acuerdas bien, lo pasó silencioso, con la cabeza escondida en el plumón. Y al entrar esta primavera, cuando el sol hacía jardín la estancia abierta y abrían las mejores rosas del patio, él quiso también engalanar la vida nueva, y cantó; pero su voz era quebradiza y asmática, como la voz de una flauta cascada.

El mayor de los niños, que lo cuidaba, viéndolo yerto en el fondo de la jaula, se ha apresurado, lloroso, a decir:

—¡Puej no l'a faltao ná, ni comida, ni agua!

No. No le ha faltado nada, Platero. Se ha muerto porque sí—diría Campoamor, otro canario viejo...

Platero, ¿habrá un paraíso de los pájaros? ¿Habrá un vergel verde sobre el cielo azul, todo en flor de rosales áureos, con almas de pájaros blancos, rosas, celestes, amarillos?

Oye: a la noche, los niños, tú y yo bajaremos el pájaro muerto al jardín. La luna está ahora llena, y a su pálida plata, el pobre cantor, en la mano cándida de Blanca, parecerá el pétalo mustio de un lirio amarillento. Y lo enterraremos en la tierra del rosal grande.

A la primavera, Platero, hemos de ver al pájaro salir del corazón de un rosa blanca. El aire fragante se pondrá canoro, y habrá por el sol de abril una errar encantado de alas invisibles y un reguero secreto de trinos claros de oro puro.

The Death of the Canary 🎶

Look here, Platero: the canary the children kept in a silver cage did not awaken this morning; he is dead. It is true that he was already quite old and feeble . . . Even last winter, you will remember how silent he seemed, how he kept his head buried beneath his soft wing. Then, when this spring came, when the sun flooded forth turning the big open room into a garden, when in the patio the best of the roses began blooming, the canary, too, wished to praise, to honor spring and the beginning of new life, and so he raised his small voice, he sang; but his voice even then was feeble and weak and sounded like a broken old flute, quivering, shaky.

When the oldest, the child who took care of him, saw him motionless, cold, stiff at the bottom of the cage, his eyes filled up with tears and he instantly cried out:

"But nothing was missing. He had his food and his water."

No. No, nothing was missing, nothing, Platero. He died because he died. As the singer Campoamor would say—another old canary.

Platero, do you think there is a paradise for birds? Do you suppose that above blue sky there might be a green garden that blossoms with golden rosebushes and blooms with the souls of the white birds, pink birds, and birds of blue and yellow?

Listen: when tonight comes, the children, you, and I will go down to the garden and take the small dead bird. The moon is full now; it sheds a pale silver light, and in Blanca's hand, white as a snowfall, the poor soft singer will appear to be nothing more than a sad and withered petal, fallen from a yellow lily in the garden, and we will bury him there beneath the large rosebush.

And when it is springtime, Platero, we shall see him, our bird, coming once more out of the heart of a lovely white rose. The air will be fragrant, filled with song, and April sunshine will be brighter with enchanted flutterings brushed by invisible soft wings, a secret trail, spun of pure shining gold, alive with a vibrant trilling.

El eco ⚜

El paraje es tan solo, que parece que siempre hay alguien por él. De vuelta de los montes, los cazadores alargan por aquí el paso y se suben por los vallados para ver más lejos. Se dice que, en sus correrías por este término, hacía noche aquí Parrales, el bandido... La roca roja está contra el naciente y, arriba, alguna cabra desviada, se recorta, a veces, contra la luna amarilla del anochecer. En la pradera, una charca que solamente seca agosto, coge pedazos de cielo amarillo, verde, rosa, ciega casi por las piedras que desde lo alto tiran los chiquillos a las ranas, o por levantar el agua en un remolino estrepitoso.

...He parado a Platero en la vuelta del camino, junto al algarrobo que cierra la entrada del prado, negro todo de sus alfanjes secos; y aumentando mi boca con mis manos, he gritado contra la roca: ¡Platero!

La roca, con respuesta seca, endulzada un poco por el contagio del agua próxima, ha dicho: ¡Platero!

Platero ha vuelto, rápido, la cabeza, irguiéndola y fortaleciéndola, y con un impulso de arrancar, se ha estremecido todo.

¡Platero!—he gritado de nuevo a la roca.

La roca de nuevo ha dicho: ¡Platero!

Platero me ha mirado, ha mirado a la roca y, remangado el labio, ha puesto un interminable rebuzno contra el cenit.

La roca ha rebuznado larga y oscuramente con él en un rebuzno paralelo al suyo, con el fin más largo.

Platero ha vuelto a rebuznar.

La roca ha vuelto a rebuznar.

Entonces, Platero, en un rudo alboroto testarudo, se ha cerrado como un día malo, ha empezado a dar vueltas con el testuz o en el suelo, queriendo romper la cabezada, huir, dejarme solo, hasta que me lo he ido trayendo con palabras bajas, y poco a poco su rebuzno se ha ido quedando sólo en su rebuzno, entre las chumberas.

The Echo ❧

In a place like this, so lonely, so deserted, it seems as if someone is always here. Returning from the hills, the hunters, as they pass through, walk faster, lengthening their stride, and climb up the stone fences to look around beyond. It is said that during his forays and attacks around these parts Parrales, the bandit, chose this place to camp for the night. A rock of red juts out against the sky at sunrise, and up there, at the top, a stray goat can be seen sometimes, his silhouette black and startling against the yellow moon. And in the meadow, a pond which dries up only in the intense heat of August catches small fragments of the sky, glitters with yellow, green, and red pieces, almost blinded by the stones thrown down to disturb the water, making it rise in whirlpools and noisy eddies.

. . . I have halted, stopped Platero at the turn of the path next to where the carob tree, standing there all in black, with its dry leathery sabers, closes up the entrance to the meadow. And I have called out, cupping my hands around my mouth, my voice resounding against the rock: "Platero!"

The rock, its answer parched and dry, although somewhat softened, sweetened by its nearness to the nearby pond and water, has called back: "Platero!"

Platero has turned his head around quickly, startled, raising it erectly, as if to fortify and defend himself, quivering with an impulse to escape, to flee.

"Platero!" I have called once again.

The rock, once again, has answered back: "Platero!"

Platero has looked then, first at me and then has looked at the rock, and curling his upper lip, throwing back his head, has let out a long, interminable braying toward the sky.

The rock has responded back, with a dark braying, a muffled braying, almost the same as Platero's long braying, yet longer, more drawn out at the end.

Platero has begun braying once more.

The rock has begun its braying once more.

Platero, then, breaking into a stubborn, rude, hardheaded uproar, closing himself off, churning like a stormy, nasty day, has begun tossing his head, whipping it in circles, or rolling on the ground to break his harness, to run away, escape, leaving me alone, until I have slowly begun to quiet him with soft words, and then, little by little, his loud braying has begun to settle down, becoming, among the cactus, his usual soft braying.

Navidad ✖

¡La candela en el campo!... Es tarde de Nochebuena, y un sol opaco y débil clarea apenas en el cielo crudo, sin nubes, todo gris en vez de todo azul, con un indefinible amarillor en el horizonte de poniente... De pronto, salta un estridente crujido de ramas verdes que empiezan a arder; luego, el humo apretado, blanco como armiño, y la llama, al fin, que limpia el humo y puebla el aire de puras lenguas momentáneas, que parecen lamerlo.

¡Oh la llama en el viento! Espíritus rosados, amarillos, malvas, azules, se pierden no sé dónde, taladrando un secreto cielo bajo; ¡y dejan un olor de ascua en el frío! ¡Campo, tibio ahora, de diciembre! ¡Invierno con cariño! ¡Nochebuena de los felices!

Las jaras vecinas se derriten. El paisaje, a través del aire caliente, tiembla y se purifica como si fuese de cristal errante. Y los niños del casero, que no tienen Nacimiento, se vienen alrededor de la candela, pobres y tristes, a calentarse las manos arrecidas, y echan en las brasas bellotas y castañas, que revientan, en un tiro.

Y se alegran luego, y saltan sobre el fuego que ya la noche va enrojeciendo, y cantan:

> ...*Camina, María,*
> *camina, José...*

Yo les traigo a Platero, y se lo doy, para que jueguen con él.

Christmas ❧

A bonfire burns in the fields! . . . The afternoon before Christmas Eve, and a pale sun, heavy and feeble, can barely give light to the sky; a raw sky, bare and cloudless, a grey sky, without a trace of blue, with an indefinable yellowish tint stretching wide along the western horizon . . . Then, suddenly, the noisy, sharp crackling of green branches, just beginning to catch fire and to burn; then, after that, the thick, curling smoke, white as ermine; and then, finally, the bright flame which clears away the smoke and begins to fill up the air with yellow and red tongues of clean, short-lived fire which seem to be touching it, licking it.

Oh, the bright flame moving in the wind! Spirits rose-colored, spirits of yellow, of mauve, and of blue, who hide themselves I know not where, piercing the secret low skyline, leaving in the cold air an odor of burning coal! Fields and meadows of December, now giving warmth! Affectionate, loving winter! Christmas Eve, for those who are happy!

The rushes, nearby, are thawing, melting. The landscape, seen through hot trembling air, wavers and shivers and becomes purified just as if made of molten, shining glass. And the children of the caretaker who have no creche come near to the fire, standing around the fire, poverty-stricken, needy and sorrowful, to warm up their cold, stiff, frozen hands and throw into the burning coals some acorns and some chestnuts which burst open with a loud pop.

And, after a while, they grow joyful and jump over the coals in the fire which the dark night has turned into a reddening glow, and they sing:

> . . . *Walk along, Mary,*
> *walk along, Joseph . . .*

I go and bring Platero, give him to the children so they may play together.

La corona de perejil 🌿

¡A ver quién llega antes!

El premio era un libro de estampas, que yo había recibido la víspera, de Viena.

—¡A ver quién llega antes a las violetas!... A la una... A las dos... ¡A las tres!

Salieron las niñas corriendo, en un alegre alboroto blanco y rosa al sol amarillo. Un instante, se oyó el silencio que el esfuerzo mudo de sus pechos abría en la mañana, la hora lenta que daba el reloj de la torre del pueblo, el menudo cantar de un mosquitito en la colina de los pinos, que llenaban los lirios azules, el venir del agua en el regato... Llegaban las niñas al primer naranjo, cuando Platero, que holgazaneaba por allí, contagiado del juego, se unió a ellas en su vivo correr. Ellas, por no perder, no pudieron protestar ni reírse siquiera...

Yo les gritaba: ¡Que gana Platero! ¡Que gana Platero!

Sí, Platero llegó a las violetas antes que ninguna, y se quedó allí, revolcándose en la arena.

Las niñas volvieron protestando sofocadas, subiéndose las medias, cogiéndose el cabello:

—¡Eso no vale! ¡Eso no vale! ¡Pues no! ¡Pues no! ¡Pues no, ea!

Les dije que aquella carrera la había ganado Platero y que era justo premiarlo de algún modo. Que bueno, que el libro, como Platero no sabía leer, se quedaría para otra carrera de ellas, pero que a Platero había que darle un premio.

Ellas, seguras ya del libro, saltaban y reían, rojas:—¡Sí! ¡Sí! ¡Sí!

Entonces, acordándome de mí mismo, pensé que Platero tendría el mejor premio en su esfuerzo, como yo en mis versos. Y cogiendo un poco de perejil del cajón de la puerta de la casera, hice una corona, y se la puse en la cabeza, honor fugaz y máximo, como a un lacedemonio.

The Wreath of Parsley 🦋

Let's see who's the first to get there!

The prize was to be a book, a book filled with pictures, which I had received just the day before, sent from Vienna.

"Let's see who's the first one to get to the violets! . . . On your mark . . . Counting one . . . two, three, go!"

Off they dashed, the lighthearted, excited little girls in whirls of pink and white, contrasting with the yellow of the sunlight. For one moment it seemed as if the mute rush of their breathing was opening up in the morning a silence through which one could hear the slow, steady striking coming from the clock in the tower of the village, the repeated buzzing of a tiny insect on the hill where there are pine trees now covered with tall, fragrant blue lilies, the gurgling of water coming from the ditch . . . It was just about the time the girls were reaching the first orange tree when Platero, who was idling around, caught the spirit of the game and decided to join them in their lively race. The girls, afraid they might lose, didn't dare stop and protest, nor even stop and laugh . . .

I called to them: "Platero is winning! Platero is winning!"

Yes, Platero reached the violets before anyone else could get there, and decided to remain, wallowing about in the dust.

The little girls came back, out of breath, out of sorts, protesting over and over, pulling up their stockings, twisting, tugging their hair:

"No, it isn't fair! No, it isn't fair! It's not fair! It's not fair! It's not fair, no way!"

I told them that Platero had won the race and that it was only fair that he be rewarded for winning and be given some sort of prize. But, since Platero was unable to read, the book would be kept and awarded to one of them as a prize in a race of their own. Nevertheless, Platero must receive a prize.

Certain of winning the book, they jumped about, their faces flushed with laughter: "Yes! Yes! Yes!"

And then, thinking about myself and how Platero would have his best reward because of this effort, just as I have found reward working on my verses, I picked a little parsley from the landlady's box near the doorway next to the house, winding it around into a wreath, and placed the wreath on Platero's head, a fleeting honor, a great honor, befitting a Spartan athlete.

Los Reyes Magos 🪷

¡Qué ilusión, esta noche, la de los niños, Platero! No era posible acostarlos. Al fin, el sueño los fue rindiendo, a uno en una butaca, a otro en el suelo, al arrimo de la chimenea, a Blanca en una silla baja, a Pepe en el poyo de la ventana, la cabeza sobre los clavos de la puerta, no fueran a pasar los Reyes... Y ahora, en el fondo de esta afuera de la vida, se siente como un gran corazón pleno y sano, el sueño de todos, vivo y mágico.

Antes de la cena, subí con todos. ¡Qué alboroto por la escalera, tan medrosa para ellos otras noches!—A mí no me da miedo de la montera, Pepe, ¿y a ti?, decía Blanca, cogida muy fuerte de mi mano.— Y pusimos en el balcón, entre las cidras, los zapatos de todos. Ahora, Platero, vamos a vestirnos Montemayor, tita, María Teresa, Lolilla, Perico, tú y yo, con sábanas y colchas y sombreros antiguos. Y a las doce, pasaremos ante la ventana de los niños en cortejo de disfraces y de luces, tocando almireces, trompetas y el caracol que está en el último cuarto. Tú irás delante conmigo, que seré Gaspar y llevaré unas barbas blancas de estopa, y llevarás, como un delantal, la bandera de Colombia, que he traído de casa de mi tío, el cónsul...

Los niños, despertados de pronto, con el sueño colgado aún, en jirones, de los ojos asombrados, se asomarán en camisa a los cristales, temblorosos y maravillados. Después, seguiremos en su sueño toda la madrugada, y mañana, cuando ya tarde, los deslumbre el cielo azul por los postigos, subirán, a medio vestir, al balcón, y serán dueños de todo el tesoro.

El año pasado nos reímos mucho. ¡Ya verás cómo nos vamos a divertir esta noche, Platero, camellito mío!

The Wise Kings 🐛

What excitement tonight, what excitement for the children, Platero! It was not possible to put them to bed, but sleep caught up with them, overcame them at last; one child fell asleep in an armchair, another on the floor next to the warmth of the fireplace, Blanca sleeping in a low chair, and Pepe by the stone seat against the wall under the window frame, his head against the nails on the door in case the Wise Men should be passing . . . And now, deep at the bottom of this, existing outside of life itself, one senses, like a giant heart, a full heart sound and healthy, the dreams of everyone, alive and magical.

Before suppertime I went upstairs with them. What a terrible racket on the stairway, so spooky and frightening to them on other nights!

"I'm not afraid of the shadows on the skylight, Pepe, are you?" Blanca was asking even as she held onto my hand tightly.

We put out everyone's shoes on the balcony, among the lemons. Now it's time, Platero; we are going to dress up, Montemayor, Tita, Maria Teresa, Lolilla, Perico, you, and I, in bed sheets and coverlets and quilts and old, battered hats. We will pass before the children's window at midnight in a parade of strange disguises and lights, bearing gifts, clanging brass mortars and playing on trumpets and blowing on the shell horn which is kept in the last room. You will be in front with me, leading the parade. I'll dress as Gaspar wearing a long white beard made out of burlap, and you will wear, as a covering, the colorful flag of Colombia which I brought for you from the house of my uncle, the Consul . . . The children, suddenly awakening, with small bits and particles of sleep still visible in their half-opened, astonished eyes, still wearing nightshirts, will peep out of the windowpane, trembling, their eyes filled with great wonder. And we will continue in their dreams later, until dawn arises. And tomorrow, when, rather late, the dazzling blue sky filtering through the shutters awakens them, they will come, half-dressed, upstairs to the balcony and will be masters of all the treasure.

Last year we laughed and laughed so much. Later on, you will see what fun we will have, what a good time we will have tonight, Platero, my little camel!

Carnaval 🎭

¡Qué guapo está hoy Platero! Es lunes de Carnaval, y los niños, que se han disfrazado vistosamente de toreros, de payasos y de majos, le han puesto el aparejo moruno, todo bordado, en rojo, verde, blanco y amarillo, de recargados arabescos.

Agua, sol y frío. Los redondos papelillos de colores van rodando paralelamente por la acera, al viento agudo de la tarde, y las máscaras, ateridas, hacen bolsillos de cualquier cosa para las manos azules.

Cuando hemos llegado a la plaza, unas mujeres vestidas de locas, con largas camisas blancas, coronados los negros y sueltos cabellos con guirnaldas de hojas verdes, han cogido a Platero en medio de su corro bullanguero y, unidas por las manos, han girado alegremente en torno de él.

Platero, indeciso, yergue las orejas, alza la cabeza y, como un alacrán cercado por el fuego, intenta, nervioso, huir por doquiera. Pero, como es tan pequeño, las locas no le temen y siguen girando, cantando y riendo a su alrededor. Los chiquillos, viéndolo cautivo, rebuznan para que él rebuzne. Toda la plaza es ya un concierto altivo de metal amarillo, de rebuznos, de risas, de coplas, de panderetas y de almireces...

Por fin, Platero, decidido igual que un hombre, rompe el corro y se viene a mí trotando y llorando, caído el lujoso aparejo. Como yo, no quiere nada con los Carnavales... No servimos para estas cosas...

Carnival ❧

How handsome Platero is today! It is Carnival Monday, and the children masquerading in colorful costumes, disguising themselves as toreadors, clowns, and hustlers, have arrayed Platero in a Moorish harness, beautifully and elaborately embroidered in red, green, white, and yellow fanciful arabesques.

Rain, sun, and cold. Small shredded round bits of confetti of every color roll and toss about, swept into long gusts flying parallel to the sidewalk by the keen-edged wind of evening, and the revelers, numb with cold, search for anything to make pockets for their frozen blue hands.

Barely have we arrived at the Square when women, masquerading as mad inmates from the insane asylum, dressed up in long white chemises, their loosened flowing black hair crowned with wreaths, intertwined with leaves of green, seize Platero and lead him into the middle of their wild merrymaking, their screaming, noisy revelry, and then, beginning to join hands, they dance and pirouette all around him in a joyful circle.

Platero, hesitatingly, pricks up his ears, raises his head, and, just like a scorpion enclosed within a flaming circle of fire, nervously tries to escape through any opening. But because he is little the crazy women do not fear him, but gyrate around him with singing and with dancing and with their wild laughter. The little children, seeing him a captive, begin to bray to encourage his braying. All of the Square is now one elegant concert, made up of clanging yellow metal, of constant braying, of popular song, of tambourines and brass mortars . . .

At last, Platero, making a firm decision like a man, breaks through the circle and comes toward me, trotting, whining, dragging half of his elegant harness on the ground. Like me, he wants nothing whatever to do with carnivals . . . We are no good for this sort of thing . . .

Afterword

MOGUER, a small Andalusian village in the south of Spain, is a place of cobblestone streets and small hills. A rise overlooks a valley. Beyond is a river, and by the river a swamp filled with reeds. To the east are mountains. In Moguer, where the sun shines all summer, there is a dazzling brightness. The low houses, whitewashed from top to bottom, reflect a sense of ease and carelessness in a place where people have all the time in the world or no time at all. It is said that there are two things the people of Moguer never know for sure: when they are going to have dinner and when they are going to die.

JUAN RAMÓN JIMÉNEZ, winner of the 1956 Nobel Prize for Literature, was born in Moguer in 1881. The son of a landowner, he was sent (as was the custom) to a Jesuit school in Cadíz when he was eleven years old. Expected to study for the law in Seville, he chose to write instead and returned to Moguer. Here, living sometimes at his childhood home Azul marino and sometimes at Fuentepina, a farm in the pinelands, he wrote *Platero y yo* in 1914. In this book of 138 chapters, Jiménez describes the wanderings of a man and his donkey through Moguer and the surrounding countryside. There is little that escaped the poet's fascination with animals, people, nature, festivals, games, birth, and death.

Nineteen of these chapters, universal in appeal, are chosen here for a literary and poetic translation—as opposed to a strictly literal translation—designed to emulate the rhythm and music of the original Spanish as well as focus attention on the keen metaphoric eye of Jiménez. For it is the poet who sees that the smudged, dirty, flushed cheeks of the coal-seller's daughter are a metaphor for lumps of burning coal. And it is the singing prose of Jiménez that haunts the reader and listener.

I am grateful to Joseph Domínguez, a native of Madrid, former college professor in Dublin and Lecturer at the Spanish/Irish Society, now living in California, for his sensitive and encouraging help in describing Moguer, for his literal translations, and for vetting the final literary translation. Many thanks to Antonio Frasconi, whose work I hang on my walls and in my heart, for his superb woodcuts, and to Dorothy Briley for publishing this book. To introduce the young to Platero in both Spanish and English has been the passion of half a lifetime.

—M.C.L.